Wallace & Gromit™

CRACKERS IN SPACE

Story and Text by
Tristan Davies

Drawings by
Nick Newman

Hodder & Stoughton

Also in the same series:
Wallace & Gromit and the Lost Slipper
Wallace & Gromit Anoraknophobia

Colouring by Tony Trimmer

First published in Great Britain in 1999 by Hodder & Stoughton
A division of Hodder Headline

10 9 8 7 6 5 4 3 2 1

A CIP catalogue record for this title is available from the British Library

ISBN 0 340 71289 9

Printed by Jarrolds Book Printing, Thetford.

Hodder & Stoughton
A division of Hodder Headline
338 Euston Road
London
NW1 3BH

Wallace & Gromit™

WALLACE: Cheese-lover, inventor, amateur rocket scientist and A Man With A Mission. As Commander, Wallace's authority is absolute. Unless anyone objects, that is. In which case his authority is… well, you get the picture.

GROMIT: With so many advanced social skills – using a knife and fork, toothbrush, etc – and his deep interest in particle physics, it is easy to forget that Gromit is a dog. But just try stealing one of his bones.

BILL 'CHEESY' CHEESEMAN: Master cheesemaker from Wensleydale and twin of the evil crime lord Rhett Leicester. As First Explosives Officer, Bill really understands the forces unleashed during the cheese fermentation process.

WENDOLENE RAMSBOTTOM (Miss): First Knitting Officer. A rare beauty whose speed-knitting skills in zero gravity conditions make her a natural choice for any Mission Implausible in deep space.

MRS BINGLEY: A paying passenger who doesn't know how to say `no' when the in-flight complimentary tea is served – and ends up wishing she had gone to Morecambe instead like last year.

WIRRAL BINGLEY: 14 next birthday, when he is not on antibiotics Wirral is a regular at the Batley Street games arcade. With Mrs B., he hopes to become the first mother and son team in space.

MR PATEL: Wallace's sensible nextdoor neighbour in West Wallaby Street who, having once been to Morecambe for the day, is ideally prepared for the role of loft-based Mission Controller.

4

9

12

14

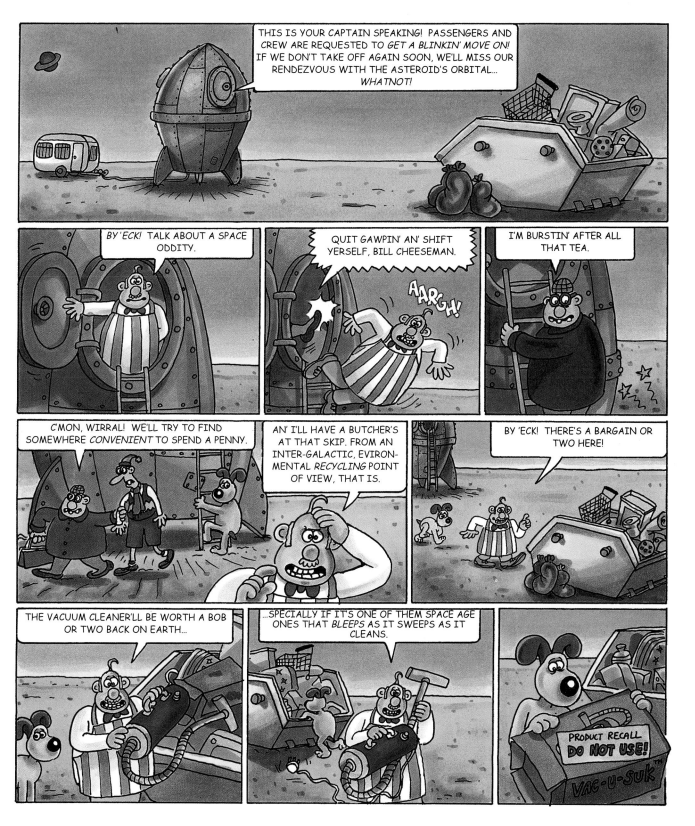

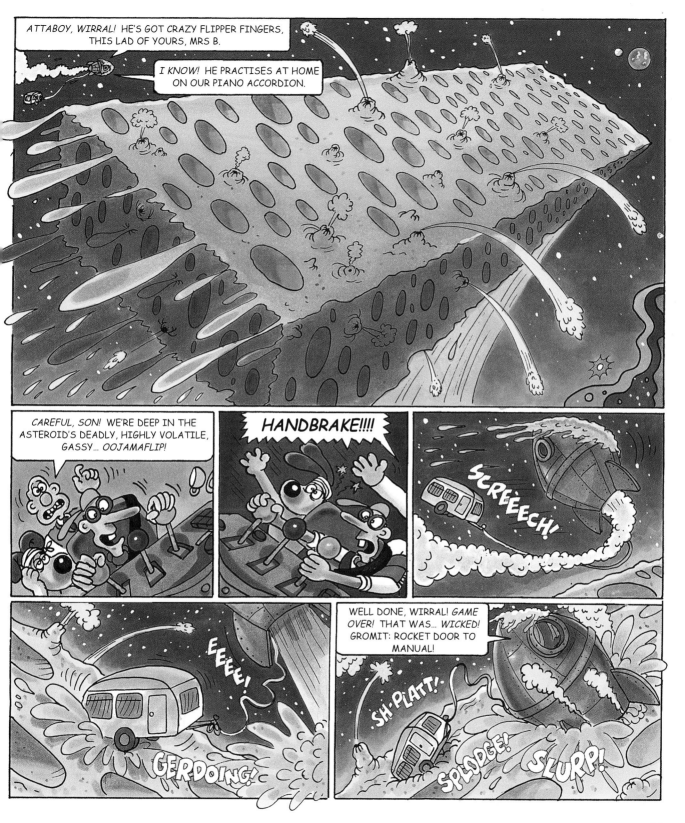

30

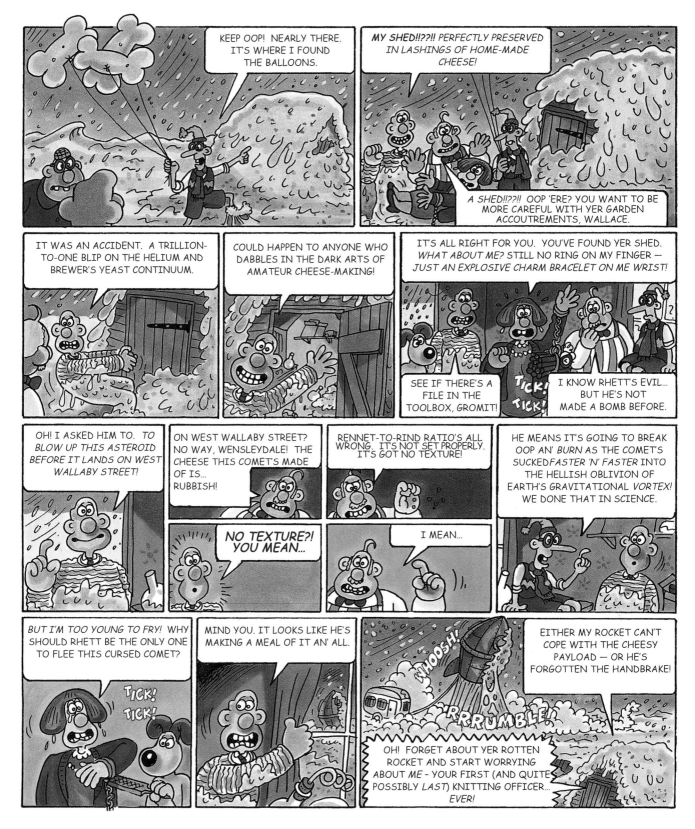

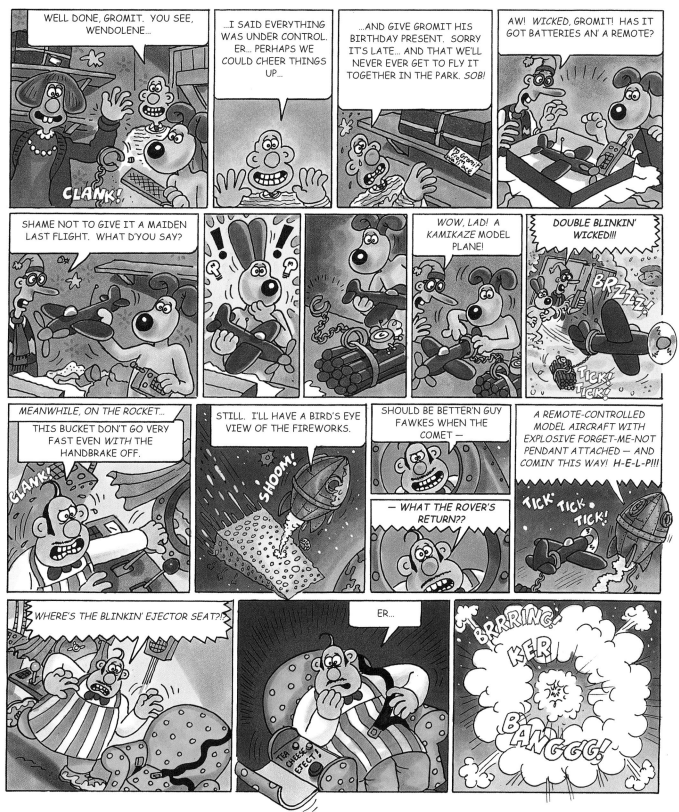

40

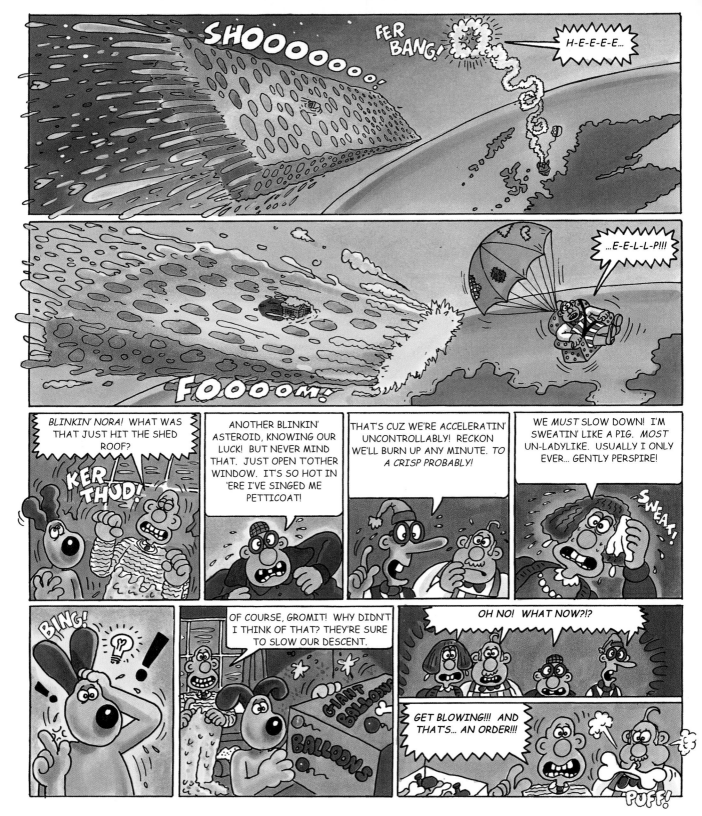

THE END

44

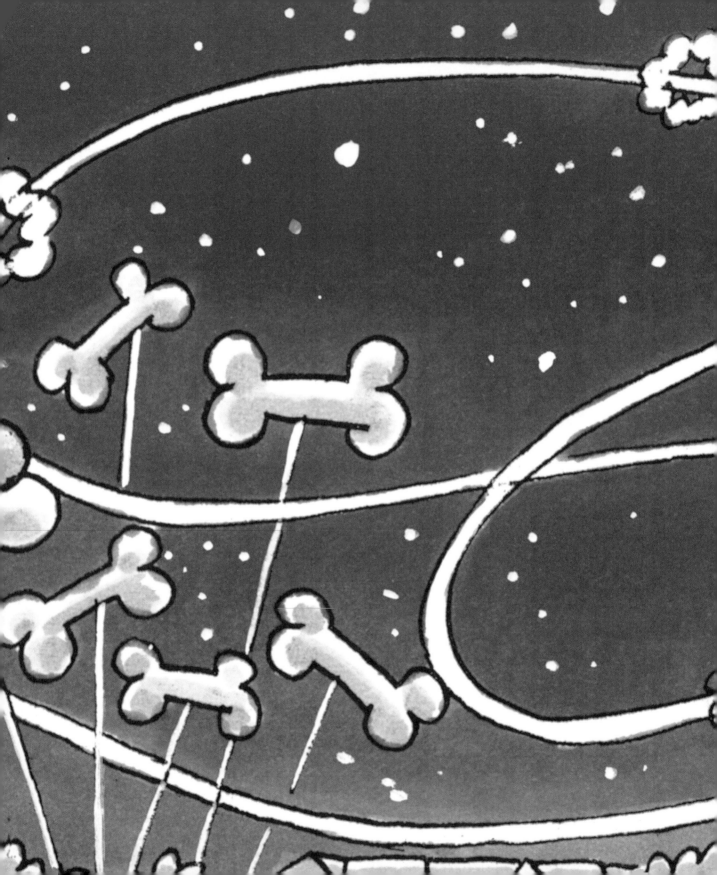